Outside My Door

 HOUGHTON MIFFLIN   BOSTON

Contents

Come and See Me

by Greg Kent

Mac Cat, Mac Cat!
Mac, Mac, Mac!

Come to me, Mac Cat.
Mac Cat sat.

Sam Cat, Sam Cat!
Sam, Sam, Sam!

Come to me.

Come to me, Sam.

Sam Cat sat.

Pam and Me

by Louise Andreas

illustrated by Judith Lanfredi

Pam, Pam, Pam, Pam!

Pam, Pam, Pam.
Come to me, Pam.

I sat. Pam Cat sat.

I pat Pam.

Pat, pat, pat.

I Can Nap

by Christopher Lawrence

 can nap.

Nap, nap, nap, nap.

I can nap with my .

Nap, nap, nap, nap.

 can nap.

Nap, nap, nap, nap.

I can nap with my .
Nap, nap, nap, nap.

Tap with Me

by Cara Blanco

illustrated by Holli Conger

I can tap.

I tap, tap, tap.

I can tap. Nan can tap.

Nan can tap, tap, tap.

I can tap with Nan.
Tap, Nan. Tap.

I am Tap Man!
Tap, tap, tap! Tap Man!

What Can You See?

by Leyla Rogers

illustrated by Shari Halpern

Cam can see a tan cat.

A tan, tan, tan cat!

Cam can see a fat tan cat.

Fan can see Jac.

Can Jac see Fan?

Jac can! Jac can!

Sam can see Nat nap.

Nap, nap, nap, Nat!

Can Mac see you?

Fat Cat

by Amy Miller

illustrated by
Hideko Takahashi

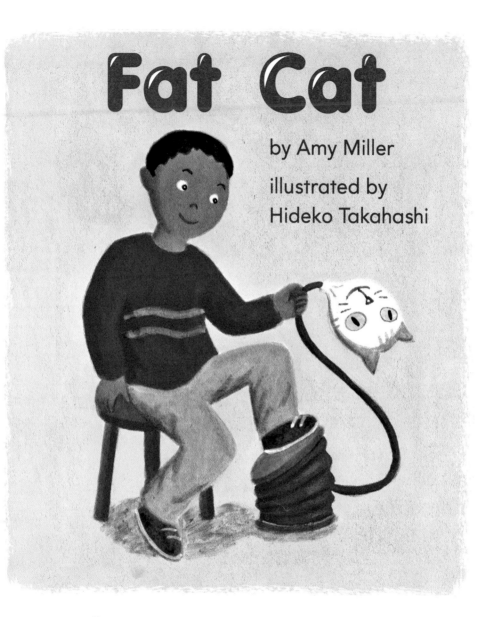

Can you see Sam?
Sam can tap, tap, tap.

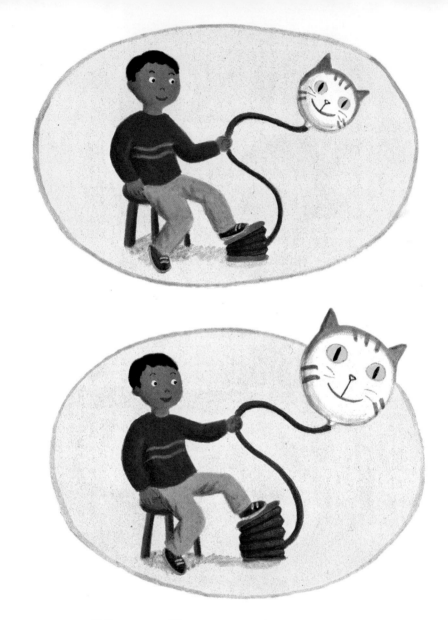

Tap, Sam, tap.

Tap, tap, tap, Sam.

Tap, Sam!

Tap. Tap. Tap.

Can you see the fat cat?
What a fat, fat, fat cat!

What Now?

by Suzanne Gerardi

Can Pam and Nan pat?

Nan can pat now.

Can Fab tap? Fab can!
Fab can tap now.

Sam and Bab are at bat.
Bat, Sam, bat!

Now we can nap, nap, nap.

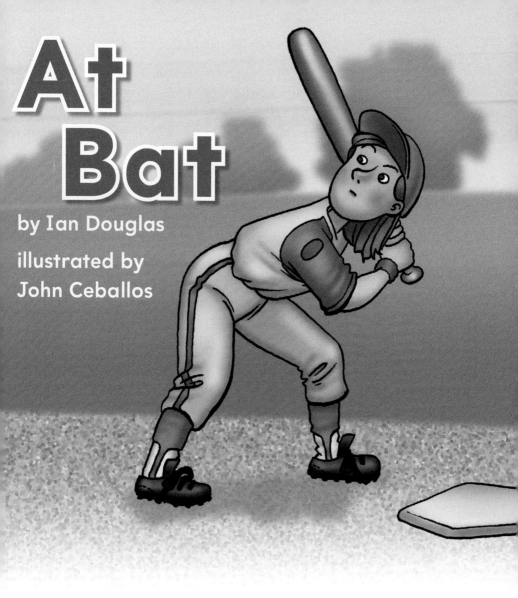

At Bat

by Ian Douglas

illustrated by
John Ceballos

See Bab at bat.

Bab can bat, bat, bat.

Bat now, Bab!
Bam!

See Pat.

Pat. Pat! Pat!

Pat! Pat! Pat! Pat!
We are , Pat!

Pam Cat

by Nina Dimopolous
illustrated by Bari Weissmann

Mac sat and sat.

Pam Cat sat.

Mac can pat Pam Cat.

Pam Cat sat, sat, sat.
Mac can fan Pam Cat.

Pam, Pam, Pam!
Come to me Pam Cat.

Come with Me

by Roger DiPaulo

illustrated by Fahimeh Amiri

Nat sat and sat.

Nat sat, sat, sat.

Come with me, Bab!
Bab! Bab! Bab!

Nat sat. Bab sat.

Nat can see Nan.

Bab can see Nan.

Nat sat. Bab sat. Nan sat.

Word Lists

I Can Nap

page 9

Decodable Words
Target Skill: *Words with n*
can, nap

High-Frequency Words
New
my, with

Previously Taught
I

Tap with Me

page 13

Decodable Words
Target Skill: *Words with n*
can, man, Nan

Words Using Previously Taught Skills
am, tap

High-Frequency Words
New
with

Previously Taught
I

What Can You See?   page 17

Decodable Words
Target Skill: *Words with f*
Fan, fat

Words Using Previously Taught Skills
big, can, nap, sip, sit, Tab

High-Frequency Words
New
you

Previously Taught
a, see

Fat Cat   page 21

Decodable Words
Target Skill: *Words with f*
fat

Words Using Previously Taught Skills
can, cat, Sam, tap

High-Frequency Words
New
what, you

Previously Taught
a, see, the

43

What Now?

Decodable Words
Target Skill: *Words with b*
Bab, bat, Fab

Words Using Previously Taught Skills
at, can, Nan, nap, Pam, pat, Sam, tap

High-Frequency Words
New
are, now

Previously Taught
and, we

At Bat

Decodable Words
Target Skill: *Words with b*
Bab, bam, bat

Words Using Previously Taught Skills
at, can, Pat

High-Frequency Words
New
are, now

Previously Taught
see, we

44

Pam Cat

Decodable Words
Target Skill: *Words with a, n, f, b*
can, cat, fan, Mac, Pam, pat, sat

High-Frequency Words
Review
and, come, me, to

Come with Me

Decodable Words
Target Skill: *Words with a, n, f, b*
Bab, can, Nan, Nat, sat

Words Using Previously Taught Skills
can, Mac, pat

High-Frequency Words
Review
and, come, me, see, with